Harry Potter™

HANDBOOK

MOVIE MAGIC

SCHOLASTIC INC.
New York   Toronto   London   Auckland   Sydney
Mexico City   New Delhi   Hong Kong

ISBN 978-0-545-29665-6

12 11 10 9 8 7 6 5 4 3 2   11 12 13 14 15 16/0

Printed in the U.S.A.   40
First printing, June 2011

CONTENTS

INTRODUCTION

The magical world that J.K. Rowling created in the *Harry Potter* book series touched the hearts and imaginations of readers around the world. When it came time to bring her vision to the big screen, producers knew they were in for a challenge. J.K. Rowling had provided countless details about the wizarding world in her books, and finding ways to bring those details to life was the biggest challenge of making the movies. From the producers to the directors to the set designers, everyone worked hard to make Rowling's vision a reality.

David Heyman, the films' producer, said, "What we were aware of was building a world. A world that was real, a world that would last, that would seem that it had been there forever, and would last forever."

Stuart Craig, the production designer, agreed: "What's pleasing about what we've done and what we're continuing to do is the number of children especially who said, 'Oh, it's just like I imagined it would be.'"

The goal was to capture the spirit of the books: "[Harry Potter and the Sorcerer's Stone is] about finding courage within yourself, being true to your friends, being loyal to your friends. If you can, find a way to let good overcome evil in your life," said Chris Columbus, the director of Harry Potter and the Sorcerer's Stone and Harry Potter and the Chamber of Secrets.

HARRY POTTER
PLAYED BY DANIEL RADCLIFFE

Casting the role of Harry Potter was one of the first steps in bringing J.K. Rowling's books to the big screen. Luckily, the casting team found the perfect actor for the part — Daniel Radcliffe.

What you may not know is that Daniel almost didn't audition for the movie! Daniel's father happened to know David Heyman, who invited him to audition for the part that would change his life.

"...I met the producer, David Heyman, in the theater one night by complete coincidence," Dan explained after *Harry Potter and the Sorcerer's Stone* was filmed. "My mum got a call from him sometime the next week asking if I'd just like to meet....not for an audition, but just to meet. We went and he was really nice, really funny. We were interested in a lot of the same things...."

Once Daniel booked the part, it didn't take him long to become friends with his co-stars, Emma Watson and Rupert Grint. **"We get along really well because we're all quite like our characters.** Rupert's very funny, Emma's very intelligent, and I'm in between because that's, I think, how Harry is."

When it came time to act in some of the more difficult scenes of the *Harry Potter* films, Daniel turned to his dad for acting advice. "I just had a really, really long discussion with my dad about [preparing for

the darker scenes in *Harry Potter and the Prisoner of Azkaban*]. He helped me so much with all the stuff with the Dementors particularly."

So, how does Dan relax between scenes? During *Harry Potter and the Prisoner of Azkaban*, he told reporters, "I watch a lot of other films, I listen to music, I read, I see my friends. Stuff like that."

HERMIONE GRANGER
PLAYED BY EMMA WATSON

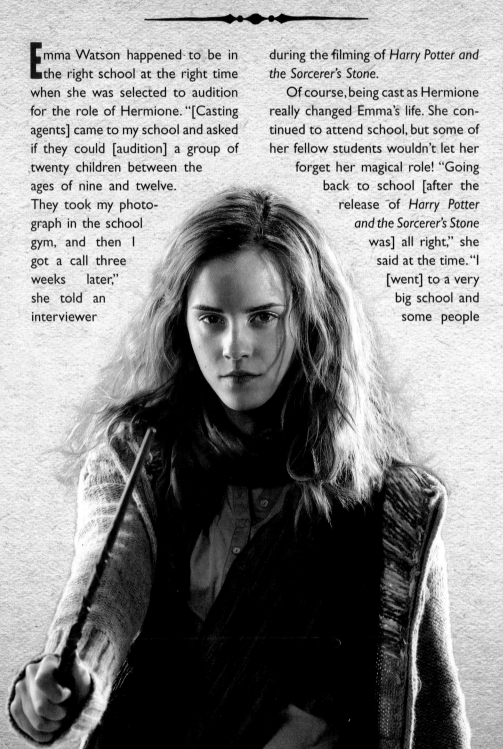

Emma Watson happened to be in the right school at the right time when she was selected to audition for the role of Hermione. "[Casting agents] came to my school and asked if they could [audition] a group of twenty children between the ages of nine and twelve. They took my photograph in the school gym, and then I got a call three weeks later," she told an interviewer during the filming of *Harry Potter and the Sorcerer's Stone*.

Of course, being cast as Hermione really changed Emma's life. She continued to attend school, but some of her fellow students wouldn't let her forget her magical role! "Going back to school [after the release of *Harry Potter and the Sorcerer's Stone* was] all right," she said at the time. "I [went] to a very big school and some people

[gave] me a bit of stick [a hard time]. They [walked] past and [would say] 'Wingardium Leviosa' for the billionth time that day, and [I'd go] 'Aaagggghhhhhh!' But apart from that **most people are really nice about it. My close friends just treat me normally."**

RON WEASLEY
PLAYED BY RUPERT GRINT

Unlike his costars, Rupert Grint auditioned the old-fashioned way. He made a videotape of himself and sent it to the casting agents. Rupert was a fan of the *Harry Potter* books, and when he heard about the movies, he was positive that he would make a great Ron Weasley. "I found out that you could audition by sending a picture of yourself and some information to Newsround," he said during the filming of *Harry Potter and the Sorcerer's Stone*. "I did my own video with me, first of all, pretending to be my drama teacher who unfortunately was a girl and then I did a rap of how I wanted to be Ron and then I made my own script thing up and sent it off."

Once the first movie was in theaters, it became a lot more difficult for Rupert to go out without being recognized! During the filming of *Harry Potter and the Chamber of Secrets*, he noted, **"People recognize me, call me Ron, and ask me questions. It's really cool and weird as well.** They usually just ask for my autograph. I've got a signature and everything. It's hard to get used to."

But being an actor has some perks, too! Filming in Scotland gave Rupert the chance to try out golf, and during the filming of *Harry Potter and the Prisoner of Azkaban*, it became his favorite hobby. "It's really good fun...Scotland is like the hometown of golf, and where we were filming there was a golf course right behind a mountain...I basically spent every night there playing golf."

Finding the right actors to play the students at Hogwarts School of Witchcraft and Wizardry was the next challenge. "We had the most fantastic group of actors, children and adults alike," David Heyman said after filming *Harry Potter and the Sorcerer's Stone*. "Once those kids got together and formed that bond, the chemistry only intensified ... They just immediately became their characters and hit it off."

DRACO MALFOY™ PLAYED BY TOM FELTON

Tom Felton took on the role of Draco Malfoy. **"I ... enjoy playing [Draco]. He's the best person to play isn't he?"** Tom told interviewers while filming *Harry Potter and the Prisoner of Azkaban*.

CHO CHANG PLAYED BY KATIE LEUNG

Katie Leung took on the role of Cho Chang, Harry's first love interest. "I wasn't really up to acting before because I didn't think I could do it," Katie said after filming *Harry Potter and the Order of the Phoenix*. "I always thought you had to be really confident to act .... Now, I think that instead of putting yourself down and not believing in yourself, if you really want something, you should go ahead and do it."

CEDRIC DIGGORY PLAYED BY ROBERT PATTINSON

The role of Cedric Diggory, one of Hogwarts' champions for the Triwizard Tournament, went to Robert Pattinson. "In the book and also my first introduction of the script is like 'an absurdly handsome seventeen-year-old' and it kind of puts you off a little bit, when you're trying to act, and you're trying to get good angles to look good-looking and stuff," Robert said at the time. "It's really stupid; you'd think I'm really egotistical. But I think that's the most daunting part about it — it's much scarier than meeting Voldemort!"

LUNA LOVEGOOD™ PLAYED BY EVANNA LYNCH

Evanna Lynch captured the role of Luna Lovegood, the eccentric Ravenclaw student. **"I used to be afraid to appear on the film set because I felt I was not ready,"** Evanna said after *Harry Potter and the Half-Blood Prince*. "But I learned that [the filmmakers] don't expect you to be perfect.... Just to be a part of the film is thrilling, because I've always been a huge fan of the books."

The main characters of the *Harry Potter* movies are Harry, Ron, and Hermione, but the adult characters — the professors, members of the Order of the Phoenix, and of course, the villains — also play a very important role in the story. Each actor had a unique take on their roles, the movies, and getting into character.

LORD VOLDEMORT™ PLAYED BY RALPH FIENNES

The role of the wizarding world's most feared Dark wizard went to Ralph Fiennes. "I hesitated for a bit before committing to the role [of Voldemort] because it sort of requires you to personify evil, and I don't know how you do that," Fiennes said of his first *Harry Potter* film, *Harry Potter and the Goblet of Fire*. **"It isn't just a creepy voice and makeup."**

PROFESSOR SEVERUS SNAPE™
PLAYED BY ALAN RICKMAN

The role of Slytherin's Head of House went to acclaimed actor Alan Rickman. "It's amazing how many people walk into the set and go around kicking the stone steps, because you can't believe that they're made out of wood," Rickman said during the filming of *Harry Potter and the Chamber of Secrets*. "It's magical, but it's also a fantastic demonstration of people's skill and that's the great joy of filmmaking of course, is that it's not a solitary activity; it's a huge team of people."

PROFESSOR ALBUS DUMBLEDORE™
PLAYED BY MICHAEL GAMBON

Michael Gambon took on the role of Dumbledore starting with *Harry Potter and the Prisoner of Azkaban*. "[Dumbledore's] got to be a bit scary," he said after *Harry Potter and the Half-Blood Prince*. **"All headmasters should be a bit scary, shouldn't they?** A top wizard like him would be intimidating. And ultimately, he's protecting Harry."

RUBEUS HAGRID™
PLAYED BY ROBBIE COLTRANE

ARGUS FILCH
PLAYED BY DAVID BRADLEY

Robbie Coltrane was selected to portray Harry's friend, the half-giant Hagrid. "Well, [playing Hagrid] was a bit sweaty, to be honest," said Coltrane after *Harry Potter and the Sorcerer's Stone*. "I had all that hair, and a huge costume that weighed over one hundred twenty pounds. Day to day, it was a bit uncomfortable, but I had a lot of fun."

David Bradley became Argus Filch, Hogwarts' caretaker. "I sat down with the costume and makeup department, and decided on a look trying on various things, and we came up with this, which looks to me like a cross between someone from the old Wild West and a medieval pickpocket," Bradley said during *Harry Potter and the Chamber of Secrets*. "All I've got to do is just pop these [teeth] in and it's an instant Filch."

Once all the key roles had been cast and the sets had been built, it was time to start filming the first movie of the series — *Harry Potter and the Sorcerer's Stone.* The adults on set were all professionals, but getting the hang of filming a movie was a challenge for the younger actors!

"It's not easy…The days are long," Emma Watson said at the time. **"It's hard work. You have to learn lines, and there are fifty billion, trillion, million things going on at the same time that you have to think about.** Like hitting your marks, getting your line right at the right time, making sure you step into the light so that your face doesn't shadow you…."

Daniel Radcliffe agreed. "It was nerve-wracking. The first day on the set, I was very nervous. I was used to rehearsing with about eight people, and then I got to the set and, including the extras, there were like a hundred and fifty people there."

Daniel, Emma, and Rupert became close friends during the first film. That friendship was especially nice when the time came to shoot the most difficult scenes in the film. Rupert and Daniel had two of the most challenging scenes in *Harry Potter and the Sorcerer's Stone.* Rupert's big scene included a life-sized game of

wizard chess that Ron, Hermione, and Harry have to play to get to the Sorcerer's Stone.

"I think the chess thing was pretty difficult because there was loads of dust everywhere and the pieces were really big," said Rupert Grint after the movie was filmed. "I got to sit on a horse, which was really fun. It was Ron's turn in the limelight because all the way through the film Harry's been the one who's been doing all the brave stuff and Ron felt a bit bad but he felt happy for Harry because he's his best friend."

Daniel's big scene came when Harry first meets Lord Voldemort — on the back of Professor Quirrell's head! Of course, Lord Voldemort's face was added in after filming, so Daniel had to act out his whole scene to the back of Professor Quirrell's [actor Ian Hart's] head. "The final chamber [scene was difficult] because that is the climax with Voldemort...it was very intense and I had to be focused," Daniel explained.

STUNTS

For the young stars, one of the coolest things about shooting *Harry Potter and the Sorcerer's Stone* was the opportunity to do some of their own stunts. They had stunt doubles for the most difficult scenes, but Rupert, Dan, and Emma each filmed the easier stunts themselves.

❧ THE TROLL SCENE ❧

Emma loved the action-packed moment in *Harry Potter and the Sorcerer's Stone* when Hermione, Harry, and Ron battle a troll in the girls' bathroom. "My favorite scene was probably the most difficult scene… the troll scene. I had to do lots and lots and lots and lots of stunts, which I think is one of the reasons I enjoyed it but one of the reasons it was so hard as well."

❧ PERIL ON ❧ THE QUIDDITCH PITCH

Daniel's biggest stunt in *Harry Potter and the Sorcerer's Stone* came when Harry's broom is jinxed during a Quidditch match, and Harry falls to the ground. **"There was one shot where I was hanging one-handed from my broomstick, twenty-two feet in the air,"** Daniel

explained after the movie was filmed. "I was wired up to the broom, with a huge airbag underneath me, and they moved me around up there. That was pretty cool."

❧ THE DEVIL'S SNARE ❧

Rupert's most challenging stunt came when Ron is caught in the Devil's Snare. **"...they lifted me up on a harness and a safety rope really, really high, and they just dropped me down into the Devil's Snare,"** Rupert told an interviewer at the time. "That was really fun, my heart stopped halfway through...."

"...we had brilliant kids, and they did really well," David Heyman said after *Harry Potter and the Sorcerer's Stone*. "They had a great time doing it. They seemed to laugh an awful lot. One of the challenges we faced was trying to stop them smiling in the middle of takes."

Life on the set of the *Harry Potter* movies was fun right from the start. Many of the young actors became friends quickly and had a great time, on and off camera! All of the kids agreed that the best scenes to film were the ones where they got to act with the other Hogwarts students. **"[Quidditch] was cool because everybody's ... whizzing 'round on the Quidditch broomsticks and everybody in the stands are cheering you,"** Daniel Radcliffe told interviewers after the movie was filmed. "They're very fun scenes to do."

But it wasn't all fun and games for the kids. They had to go to school every day on set. It was tough work to complete all their schoolwork and film scenes, but it was important to the actors that they continue their education. "We had a tutor on the set," Rupert explained during *Harry Potter and the Sorcerer's Stone.*

"Whenever we weren't filming, we were in the classroom studying. We had to study a minimum of three hours and a maximum of five hours a day."

Daniel found the perks to going to school on set: "There was a private tutor for all of us and we would get as much as five hours a day of school but there was no homework or detentions!"

THE SETS

Although many sets were constructed for the first film, set designers had to build many locations for the second movie. It was very important to Chris Columbus, the director of the first two *Harry Potter* movies, that the sets feel like real places. He certainly succeeded! Many fans would love the chance to explore the sets.

"Hogwarts is a place that should look as if it's been built by magic ... constructed by magic," Columbus said. "At the same time it had to feel timeless, it had to feel as if it's existed forever. It had to be sort of a little grungy, a little dirty, but it still had to have some integrity. You feel like you're at the school, which

is a remarkable achievement from our production designer."

The real challenge was that Hogwarts is not only magical, but very old. In order to recreate Hogwarts, Production Designer Stuart Craig and his team built the sets from the ground up and created many of the props with plastic. They made beams, walls, and even furniture that way. "The chief

material used in the set construction on this film [*Harry Potter and the Chamber of Secrets*] was plastic," Craig explained. "They make molds, impressions of real things, and then out of those molds, a cast of solid sheets of brickwork, sculptures, you know, oak beams, whatever you need."

SPECIAL EFFECTS

Harry Potter and the Chamber of Secrets required more advanced special effects than the first film, which meant that the actors had their work cut out for them. They had to perform in front of green screens for many scenes. Green screens allow the special effects crew to add in the cool creatures and fireworks from spells.

DANIEL ❧ AND DOBBY ❧

Daniel Radcliffe had some of the most difficult special effects scenes. He had several key scenes with Dobby the house-elf. Dobby was created using CGI (computer-generated imagery), which means he was created entirely on a computer. It was a real acting challenge for Dan!

"I think the hardest part to direct for Dan and myself was Dan's interaction with Dobby because he didn't have anyone in the room," said Chris Columbus, the film's director. "He was basically acting with a little green ball at the end of a stick.... but, **Dan was so focused, he made you believe that Dobby was there**."

❧ SPOOKY SPIDERS ❧

In some cases, the filmmakers used real creatures and enhanced them after the fact, or they created large prop replicas. Rupert Grint had to shoot a particularly tough scene with a very large spider. "[Harry and Ron] come into the spider's hollow, and then [we meet] Aragog — a spider that is the size of an elephant ...." Rupert said during filming. "I'm really scared of spiders. That didn't help my fear at all."

❧ FLYING CAR ❧

John Richardson was the Special Effects Supervisor on the film. His job was to bring all of the effects to life. He tried to avoid CGI wherever possible because he wanted everything in the films to feel very real. His favorite creation was the flying car. "It really flew!" Richardson exclaimed. "Up to the window, opened its boot [trunk] for the children's luggage, waited for them to get in, flew away."

John and his team achieved this magical effect by using a miniature model version of the car that was remotely linked to the full-size vehicle. When they moved the miniature version on a miniature set, the life-size car would also move. The end result...a flying car!

STUNTS

Of course, all those special effects meant extra stunt work for the actors. Rupert especially had some fun stunts in *Harry Potter and the Chamber of Secrets*. "[The] Whomping Willow scene…is really fun because it's like a theme park ride and I got to drive a car," Rupert exclaimed. [He was thirteen at the time.]

One of Rupert's special effects scenes posed a different challenge. "Ron has a scene where he has to cough up these giant slugs," Rupert said. **"I had this giant slug in my mouth loaded with slime and I spat [it] out. I think it was plastic. I hope it was plastic."**

For Daniel, the stunts became much more athletic. He had to do a lot of running, jumping, and fighting — which was okay with him. "Action scenes are so much fun," Daniel said. **"In one of the car scenes I was actually hanging out of the door ... thirty-five feet up in the air, which was really cool. I do most of my stunts myself."** The downside? "It's true I had to exercise a lot more…for the climbing and sword-fighting scenes," Daniel confessed.

Emma had fewer action scenes than Rupert or Daniel, but she did get a chance to try out some amazing special effects makeup when Hermione drinks Polyjuice Potion and turns into a cat!

As the cast prepared to film the third *Harry Potter* movie, they were facing a lot of changes. Richard Harris, who played Dumbledore in the first two films, passed away. Michael Gambon stepped into the role. Everyone was very sad to lose Richard, but Michael brought a new perspective to the role and quickly made it his own.

Richard Harris

Michael Gambon

"Well, obviously it was quite hard to replace Richard Harris," Rupert Grint said after the movie was filmed. "He was so brilliant for the role and it was really sad to see him go, but this new guy Michael Gambon, he's really good. He's really brought something else to the role."

There was another new actor on set as well. Gary Oldman played Sirius Black, an escaped convict who also happens to be Harry's godfather. "He brings a real depth and humanity to Sirius Black, who is a complex character," David Heyman said of the new cast member. "He's been locked up for twelve years in Azkaban prison, and now he's escaped. He is

in many ways the father Harry never had."

"...there's something incredibly magnetic about Gary," Daniel Radcliffe said after filming *Harry Potter and the Order of the Phoenix*. "I just think it's his

intensity. It's a constant process of refinement when you work with him…With Gary you could do one hundred takes and every time he's trying to get it better and better. He's fearless."

One last big change on the set — a new director! Chris Columbus directed the first two films, but Alfonso Cuarón took the helm for *Harry Potter and the Prisoner of Azkaban*. It was a darker film than the first two films, and Alfonso was well suited for the more mature storyline.

"Everything we learned with Chris over two years — which was a lot — we [got] a chance to put it into practice with another director," Daniel said. "That was a challenge in itself, because we had to get used to someone else's style, but it has helped us a lot to evolve or develop just making the transition."

Emma Watson agreed. "Especially for me, as someone who hasn't acted in anything else before, it was great working with a new director and doing something different, seeing different techniques, different ideas," she said after filming. "It's also been really good fun…."

ANIMAL ADVENTURES

Harry Potter and the Prisoner of Azkaban focused more on animals than the previous two movies, which meant the cast spent more time with their feathered or furry cast mates. Gary Gero's Birds & Animals Unlimited were the animal trainers for all the *Harry Potter* movies. Gary knew just how to get his animal actors to give superb performances.

❧ CATS ❧

Emma loved the cat playing Crookshanks almost as much as Hermione loved Crookshanks in the films! "Oh, I love my cat! [Dan and Rupert] are so rude to my cat... Okay, so it's got a flat nose... It's beautiful in its own ugly way."

There was another cat at Hogwarts that wasn't so lovable — Argus Filch's resident spy, Mrs. Norris. "... Mrs. Norris is in her second movie," Gary Gero said at the time. "She's had two years of training now, and she's becoming a fairly sophisticated old hand at this."

❧ BATS AND RATS ❧

Working with cats sounds fun, but what about working with bats, rats, mice, and lizards? "A bat landed on my head," Daniel said after the movie was shot. "It was actually very funny. I actually really love the animals, especially the lizards. The lizards are so cool. And the mice are fighting [on the set] — the mice are fantastic. We're taking bets on them. It's between who's going to win or who's going to escape first."

The role of Scabbers, Ron's pet rat, was pivotal to the third film. "There are three Scabbers, depending on how animated they want Scabbers to be," said Gary Gero. **"[Rats] are very intelligent little animals.** They learn simple things really quickly."

❧ OWLS ❧

Owls play a very important role in all the *Harry Potter* movies. The trainers were able to bring some of the more important owls, like Hedwig, to life with some very intelligent birds. "There really is just one Hedwig — his real name is Gizmo," explained Gary Gero. "He has a couple of helpers that help him out with different things."

And what about Errol, the owl belonging to the Weasley family? "He's a silly character, and he runs into everything," Gary Gero said. "He flies and crashes into bowls of potato chips. We had to teach him not only to fly and carry letters … but we also had to teach him how to lie on his back and get up from lying on his back …. **[Owls are] wonderful creatures …. They get very dedicated to you."**

FACING EVIL

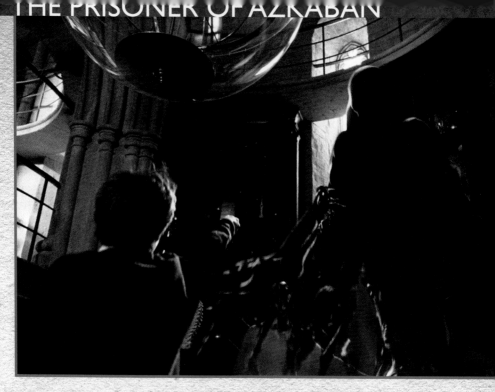

Harry Potter and the Prisoner of Azkaban has villains you love to hate, plus some surprise twists that reveal unlikely heroes and unforeseen dangers. Bringing the bad guys to life on screen was a lot of hard work for the entire cast and crew. But sometimes it pays to be bad!

❧ SLAP HAPPY ❧

Tom Felton played Draco Malfoy, and, as much as he loved his character, he also loved that Draco got a taste of his own medicine in *Harry Potter and the Prisoner of Azkaban*. "I quite like the scene where we're up in the hills and I was spying on Hagrid when they're about to slice the Hippogriff's head off, and Hermione comes up and, err, teaches [Draco] a lesson," Tom said after filming.

THE DEMENTORS

The Dementors play a big role in *Harry Potter and the Prisoner of Azkaban*, but during the filming, the actors weren't sure how the Dementors would look. "Alfonso described [the Dementors] to [Emma, Rupert and Dan] very, very vividly, and they ain't … pretty," Daniel Radcliffe said after filming. "They're [going to be] really horrific. **I think they're the scariest things in all the *Harry Potter* books.**"

For Rupert, it could be a challenge to film against a green screen. "It's weird [filming scenes and not knowing the final result of how the scenes will look] — and there's some scary puppet stuff as well," he reflected during the movie's making. "Yeah, it's really weird doing all the special effects stuff, but it's really satisfying to see it all at the end."

THE SHRIEKING SHACK

Most of the big twists and turns in the third film happened in the Shrieking Shack. Getting the look of that set perfect was crucial to setting the tone of those scenes. "The most interesting scene [in *Harry Potter and the Prisoner of Azkaban*] is probably the Shrieking Shack . . ." Daniel said. "[The] walls actually leaned and creaked, so we couldn't actually hear what each other was saying."

THE GOBLET OF FIRE™

FAVORITE SCENES

With the return of Voldemort and the death of a Hogwarts student, *Harry Potter and the Goblet of Fire* was much darker than any of the previous movies. Mike Newell stepped in to direct the film. It was very important to him to balance the darker subject matter with funny details and lots of great action scenes. He also played up the competition and magical challenges of the Triwizard Tournament™, making viewers feel like they were right in the middle of the action.

THE QUIDDITCH™
❧ WORLD CUP ❧

One of Rupert's favorite scenes to film was the Quidditch World Cup. "There was a campfire scene where we did a big night shoot and they had thousands of these tents," he said during filming. **"At one point, there are attacks at the campsites,** and there were explosions going off and fire everywhere and everyone was running about .... It was a fun scene to do."

UNDERWATER IN THE LAKE

The second task in the Triwizard Tournament was filmed in a large "green screen" diving tank. Daniel Radcliffe and Robert Pattinson had to spend a lot of time underwater to get the scenes just right. Daniel's swimming motions were animated with a CG double. His fishy appearance, plus the murky water, rocks, and plants, were completely computer generated.

"I think I was doing the underwater stuff for about two months ...." Robert said at the time. "...I did about three weeks of learning how to scuba dive."

THE AMAZING MAZE

One of Robert's favorite scenes was filmed in the maze for the final challenge in the Triwizard Tournament. "I liked the maze part .... A lot of it was on Steadicam — which is just a guy running around with a camera — and all the hedges moved. So me and Dan were basically chasing each other around and punching each other, with these hedges squeezing us .... It was really fun. There were lots of cuts and bruises afterward, and it felt like you were doing a proper job!"

TRIWIZARD TOURNAMENT

THE FIRST TASK:
COLLECTING THE
❖ GOLDEN EGG ❖

The large crowd in the arena was a combination of live-action and CGI. There were live spectators in the stands, but the lower part of the arena was computer generated. The dragons were created using models that were made larger with computer editing. It took a long time to get them to look as ferocious and frightening as they do in the movie.

"For the dragon, we started with a cyber scan of a quarter-scale maquette [scale model]," said Tim Alexander, one of the special effects supervisors for the movie. "We found out that we couldn't get the exact right shape on the tail.... So, we went back and sculpted extra details on the model."

THE SECOND TASK:
UNDERWATER
❖ RESCUE ❖

For the second task, many underwater creatures had to be created digitally, including the merpeople and Grindylows. "We met a great challenge with the Grindylows, as these octopus-like creatures come in swarms," explained Tim Webber, another visual effects supervisor. "We developed a piece of software ... that allowed us to use hand animation while manipulating huge numbers of models."

THE THIRD TASK:
❧ THE MAZE ❧

To win the Triwizard Cup, the four champions had to fight their way through a moving maze of hedges with magical traps. The crew tried using motorized hedges, but it was too difficult to get the shots to look right. So in the end, they filmed the cast on a blue screen and filled in all the hedges and creatures on computers. "We were receiving shots with just the kids on blue screen," Nicolas Aithadi, a CG supervisor, told interviewers. "We had to recreate everything behind and in front of them."

❧ THE DARK ❧ LORD RETURNS

When Harry and Cedric are transported by Portkey to the graveyard, Voldemort makes his return — growing out of a cauldron using computer-generated effects. It needed to look creepy and frightening, and using digital effects allowed the crew to really make the moment stand out! "We divided the shot into separate elements: the cauldron, the cauldron smoke, the cloak smoke, the cloak, the fire, the slime, the drips and Voldemort," Aithadi explained. **"Voldemort alone was quite complex, as the effect included skin, wet skin, bones, organs, and muscles."**

MAGICAL FRIENDSHIPS

Robert Pattinson played Cedric Diggory, Harry's competitor in the Triwizard Tournament and for the heart of Cho Chang. "I think [Cedric's] a pretty cool character," Robert said during filming. "He's not really a complete cliché of the good kid in school. He's just quiet. He is actually just a genuinely good person, but he doesn't make a big deal about it or anything…I can kind of relate to that."

❧ THE YULE BALL: ❧ A MAGICAL EVENING

Filming the Yule Ball was a lot of fun for the cast and crew. There were a few romantic moments to capture — and plenty of awkward ones, too! Hermione, especially, comes into her own in the Yule Ball scenes. She wears a gorgeous dress and dances with Viktor Krum. "I didn't know there were so many ways that you could walk down stairs actually until that day and it was difficult," Emma said after the movie was shot. "Mike [the director] was giving me all these directions, 'Keep your head up, make sure your back is straight, but don't make it too frumpy, glide smoothly.' By the time we did it, I was an absolute wreck!"

For the last four *Harry Potter* films, David Yates stepped in to direct. He jumped at the chance to bring the last three Harry Potter books to life on the big screen. "I was involved with the script [*Harry Potter and the Order of Phoenix*] for a year and a half before we started shooting," Yates said. "I sort of made the film before I shot a single frame of film really because I had so

long to prepare it. I storyboarded very carefully. By the time I got to the floor to direct the first shot on the first day, I'd already made the film three times over in my head. I think that made the studio and the producers much more comfortable, so once I started shooting they let me get on with it."

❧ GIRL POWER ❧

In *Harry Potter and the Order of the Phoenix*, the female characters really stand out. Hermione and Luna help lead Harry toward the most practical and sensible solutions. Ginny Weasley proves herself to be very courageous. As for Dolores Umbridge, her actions show that not all villains are male.

"I'm a bit of a feminist," Emma Watson said after filming the movie. **"It's really important to stand up for yourself, whether you're a girl or a boy.** But that's also true for Hermione because she's never afraid to take control of a situation or be the brains behind anything. She says what she thinks and doesn't hold back. In many ways, she bosses the boys around, which I think is kind of cool. I think they need her. That's girl power."

"Luna seems small and young and not noted for being brave, and yet she is," Evanna Lynch said of her character. "She's really calm though, she doesn't get surprised by anything, and she accepts people's differences. In fact, J. K. Rowling told me as a character she's the most adjusted to the idea of death in the whole series . . . . She'll take it as it comes."

❧ **FACING THE PAST** ❧

Harry and Neville Longbottom both suffer emotionally because of Lord Voldemort's past actions against their families. But when they gather their friends to form Dumbledore's Army, they face their pasts and decide who they wish to be in the future.

"Well, Neville's not as soft as he was in the first four films," Matthew Lewis said of Neville. "He's very shy and vulner-able…But when Harry reinstates Dumbledore's Army in this film, Neville really has something to fight for. He hates Voldemort because [Voldemort] took his parents away from him. And although he's still terrified and he has no idea how he's going to help, he knows he has to help in some way. So you really get to see another side to Neville that's very courageous and honorable."

Harry's relationship with Professor Dumbledore also evolves as they each prepare for upcoming battles

against Voldemort. **"The relationship between Harry and Dumbledore gets really interesting [in this film] because of fear,"** Daniel told interviewers during the movie's filming. "Dumbledore thinks Voldemort might be using Harry's eyes to see what [Harry's] seeing. And so Dumbledore ends up ignoring Harry at the time when Harry needs him most."

❧ MAJOR MAKEUP ❧

A lot of the effects in *Harry Potter and the Order of the Phoenix* were done digitally, but many were done using special effects makeup, prosthetics, and other real-life props.

"We did this scene where I had to be splattered with a lot of gunk from this cactus [Mimbulus mimbletonia] that Neville has, and David, the director, wanted me to do it in such a way

that I had to stay perfectly still when this stuff splattered me," said Matthew Lewis. **"He thought it would be funnier if there were no reaction from Neville whatsoever. So I just got hit in the face and I had to act stunned.** But because this thing came out so quickly, I jumped back from it every time we tried to shoot the scene. And the more I did it, the more frustrated I got and the more I jumped. It

was really embarrassing. Every time I did it, they had to get me a new jumper and get me washed because I was covered in green sludge. But we got through it in the end."

Another challenge was Mad-Eye Moody's mad eye. "We did…a major multipiece silicone prosthetic makeup for Brendan Gleeson, with an animatronic, radio-controlled eye," said Nick Dudman, the Makeup Effects Designer.

Lord Voldemort's look was also quite complicated. "Although Ralph Fiennes's nose is removed digitally, everything else on him is real, so we do prosthetic pieces for his forehead, take out his eyebrows, cover all visible skin with a network of transferred veins, which are done on a temporary tattoo system. It's printed out on a computer so we can line them all up identically every day," Dudman explained.

DUMBLEDORE'S ARMY

In *Harry Potter and the Order of the Phoenix*, a group of students at Hogwarts form Dumbledore's Army to train in Defense Against the Dark Arts. And as the characters grow up, their relationships become more complicated as well. Harry has his first romance, his first kiss, and his first broken heart — all while preparing for battle!

"Harry becomes a teacher, using all the knowledge that he's gained over the last five years to try and train as many other people as he can how to fight because he knows that Voldemort is back," Daniel said of his character's evolution in the movie. "He knows there is a war coming. And so he knows that if Hogwarts

there training and doing spells. I had a wand and people were in harnesses and were flying about the room. Even the kissing scene was in there. And I enjoyed that a lot! **It's not very often that you kiss somebody and there are tons of people watching you.** So that was a bit nerve-wracking. But after I did it, I felt like I could conquer the world."

isn't teaching its students what they need to know, they won't stand a chance against everything that's about to happen. So he puts together a training group called Dumbledore's Army. At first, he's a really reluctant teacher. Hermione talks him into it. As usual, Hermione's right."

"Most of [Cho's] scenes were based in the Room of Requirement," said Katie Leung, who plays Cho Chang. "I had so much fun. Everyone was involved. All the kids were in

"I was slightly nervous [about Harry and Cho's kiss] because I knew Katie was [nervous]," Daniel said after the movie was filmed. "There was lots of courtesy chewing gum going in my mouth that day. But it's odd. It's quite a clinical sort of thing because you're there and you'll sort of be in the kissing position and someone will say, 'Dan, move to your right.'"

Harry Potter and the Half-Blood Prince takes place during Harry's sixth year at Hogwarts. Like all of the films, it is full of magic, action, and danger. However, there is also a lot of romance, and everyone's favorite magical sport — Quidditch!

❧ SNOGGING ❧

"The way [Ginny and Harry's first kiss] was done was very romantic," said Bonnie Wright, who plays Ginny Weasley, after the movie was filmed. "Daniel and I have always been good friends, which I think worked in our favor.... My character initiates the kiss, which is great because it gives this power to girls and shows that it's okay to be the one who makes the approach."

What about Daniel? "I do think people responded to the fact that there was kissing and hormones and all that kind of stuff," he said on the *Harry Potter and the Half-Blood Prince* set.

And there was a love interest for Ron too. "[Ron and Lavender's first kiss] was kind of a big moment," Rupert Grint said during filming. "We were both quite nervous about it because we were in a room full of people who were shouting at us. It was a little bit embarrassing, but it was quite a bit of fun, too."

🎀 QUIDDITCH 🎀

There was no Quidditch in *Harry Potter and the Order of the Phoenix,* so the cast was excited to take to the skies again. But the scenes could be quite challenging. "Quidditch is quite hard," Rupert told interviewers during filming. **"I was surprised at how physical it is 'cause we had to do quite a bit of training on a trampoline which was actually quite scary.... They** rigged us up to this wire rig and we had to do flips and stuff...." But Rupert's fellow actors thought highly of his performance. "In terms of the comedy, [this film] is Rupert's finest hour," Daniel said. "He's absolutely brilliant in the movie.... You balance the dramatic stuff as well, but the scene on the broomstick in Quidditch is some-

thing.... It's absolutely brilliant."

"I've never done any of those [Quidditch] stunts before," said Bonnie Wright during the filming. "We were up ten to twenty feet in the sky on our brooms. We're not as high up as they are in a real game of Quidditch, but it's quite demanding. They turn you around and make you go fast and spin. It was a lot of fun."

GROWING UP

In *Harry Potter and the Half-Blood Prince*, the characters face dark forces, choose sides, and decide what type of wizards and witches they want to be. Portraying characters going through such tumultuous times was challenging for the actors, but it also gave them a chance to test their acting skills.

❧ HERMIONE ❧

"...in the film you see quite a strong Hermione, quite a girl power Hermione. She's the brains behind

her — to keep her energy and to keep her growing and upbeat," said Bonnie Wright.

the operation, but...you see a very different Hermione [too]," Emma Watson said on the set. "She's much more fragile and vulnerable and emotional. She's experiencing her first heartache.... So it was a challenge for me to play this much more emotional and vulnerable person."

❧ DRACO ❧

"This was a great opportunity for me to dive a little bit deeper into Draco's head and discover that

❧ GINNY ❧

"I think the biggest challenge [playing Ginny] is probably just to play her as Jo Rowling has written

he really is a coward through and through," Tom Felton said during the filming of *Harry Potter and the Half-Blood Prince*. "So it was fun to explore a bit deeper and make him more fundamentally three-dimensional."

❧ HARRY ❧

"The big change for Harry [in *Harry Potter and the Half-Blood Prince*] is his relationship with Dumbledore," Daniel explained on the set. "Previously it's always been very much teacher and student. This year it kind of changes it to being his general, a favorite lieutenant. Harry's become a foot soldier and is happy to be so. Also…he's actually being proactive and planning, actually trying to do something towards the ultimate destruction of Voldemort."

❧ DUMBLEDORE'S DEATH ❧

Of course, some scenes were very difficult to film. Dumbledore's death was an intense scene for the actors. "**[Filming the scene with Dumbledore's death] was really shocking and sad…**" said Bonnie Wright. "[It] was probably the hardest one for everyone to shoot."

"It's a very moving scene," said Warwick Davis, who plays Professor Flitwick. "When you've been so close to all the characters and then have to stand there and witness [Dumbledore's death] it was really quite, quite moving for me personally as well as in a character sense."

CREATING THE CAVE

For Dumbledore and Harry's journey to find the Horcrux in the cave, the props and special effects department pulled out all the stops. They had to create the cave, the lake, the pedestal, and Horcrux, plus the Inferi waiting just under the water. The most challenging part of the entire sequence was lighting the Inferi on fire.

"We all have a feeling about how [Inferi] should be and what they look like," said David Heyman. "And so to come up with something that had a connection to [Inferi] of the upper world, but that was unique to water, that was the most difficult."

"[The Inferi are] certainly much bolder and scarier than we imagined that they'd ever go in a *Potter* movie," explained Tim Alexander, the visual effects supervisor. "Director David Yates was really cautious of not making this into a zombie movie… A lot of it came down to their movement — they don't move fast, but they don't move really slow or groan and moan. We ended up going with a very realistic style."

Harry Potter and the Deathly Hallows–Part I is the first film where most of the scenes don't take place at Hogwarts. It chronicles the first half of the seventh book in the series, and it focuses on Harry, Ron, and Hermione's journey to find Voldemort's Horcruxes. The actors were all excited to film such a different movie, but it was bittersweet, too. They were coming to the end of years of working together. "It's been amazing to keep the core group of us here since the beginning," said Bonnie Wright. "No one's been left or changed. I think that dynamic has developed year to year."

Yet there were some things that the cast wasn't sad to leave behind. "[About my Hogwarts uniform,] I was like, 'Burn it!'" exclaimed Emma Watson. "Oh, my God, to be done with those shoes and that uniform — that was an exciting day."

There was also the challenge of filming the darker scenes in the book. "...David [Yates, director] as well as Steve Kloves [screenwriter] haven't shied away from the more severe stuff," said Matthew Lewis.

"...I'm so excited about the seventh film...we are doing something very, very different," said Daniel Radcliffe. **"We're not at Hogwarts. The difference that makes is extraordinary."**

DARKNESS FALLS

Harry Potter and the Deathly Hallows–Part I is an edgier, darker film than the previous *Harry Potter* movies. As Lord Voldemort continues to gain power in the wizarding world, tensions rise, and the imminent peril of the wizarding community becomes apparent. It was up to the actors to bring those feelings of danger and suspense to life on screen.

"It's going to feel very real," said David Yates. "We're going for a verité [realistic] approach. Being away from Hogwarts, [Harry, Ron, and Hermione are] like these three refugees on the run. They're out in the big bad world, facing real danger, unguarded by those wonderful benign wizards at Hogwarts. They don't have a home to go to. We're kind of pulling away from the magic a bit and bringing more reality to it."

"It's pretty unrelenting," Daniel Radcliffe stated. "The first half of the film is…very emotional. The whole film is about faith and about how far can it be tested — Harry's faith in Dumbledore — how far can that be stretched."

"[Harry, Ron, and Hermione are] paranoid. **It's quite a scary world because the Snatchers and Death Eaters are running around everywhere,**" Rupert Grint explained. "Harry, Ron, and Hermione are just camping out in random places, living rough, in regular clothes. Me and Dan actually have some stubble."

The final film in the *Harry Potter* series is all about the final battle at Hogwarts, when Harry faces Lord Voldemort. The cast and crew knew they had to deliver something truly epic for the final film. To give the scenes life and depth, the filmmakers decided to take advantage of new 3-D technology to put viewers right in the middle of the action.

"I am obviously looking forward to some of the battle sequences in the second part," said David Yates. "I am also looking forward to seeing the dragon flying up. I think there's a lot that will be great in 3-D, but to me, where it's really most exciting is just making that world seem much deeper, richer and what that extra dimension gives you."

"I think [the characters] all know the ending," Evanna Lynch told interviewers. "They all know that it has to come. And they all have an idea that

the more subtle stuff. 'Cause at the end of the day, as much fun as all that is, there's also the idea that it is a war going on and people are dying."

The sets also took on a new level of importance for the final film. Sets are always instrumental to creating the right look and tone of a scene, but in the final film, they were crucial to establishing that the wizarding world was facing very grim and dangerous times. And, as the battle scenes were filmed, many sets were destroyed.

Harry's not going to be there. They all jump in. They go back to form Dumbledore's Army, and they're ready. They don't need Harry as much anymore. I think for Luna, personally, she's really happy because in [*Harry Potter and the Half-Blood Prince*] she established she has friends, so that's all she needs to fight."

"Neville's taken on a much bigger role this year and it's been so much fun to do," said Matthew Lewis. "I've had a lot more scenes to do, and tougher scenes as well. Not just physically. **Some of the stuff stunt-wise and the physicality of some of the bigger action sequences are tough**, but I've enjoyed that, but then also

Every fan wants to feel like they have closure with the characters they've read about and watched for so many years, and bringing those moments to their proper conclusion on the big screen was very important to the filmmakers and cast.

RELATIONSHIPS RESOLVED

"I have to kiss Emma Watson, which was a bit weird," Rupert Grint confessed. "I've known her since she was nine. It just felt wrong really, but it was fine in the end and I think it's quite sweet."

"Rupert and I...were so desperate to get it out of the way," Emma said. "Rupert and I felt the pressure of this kiss. There's so much media interest and also the fans, this is like ten years' worth of tension and hormones and chemistry, everything in like one moment. We had to ace it."

For Evanna Lynch, one of the most exciting parts was exploring Luna's home life. "It was brilliant [filming with Rhys Ifans, who plays Luna's father, Xenophilius Lovegood] because he's really so happy just being by himself. He's really honest too, as well."

For Helena Bonham Carter, who

plays Voldemort's loyal follower, Bellatrix Lestrange, one of the most entertaining parts of the movie was having the chance to break out of character. "...Hermione takes Polyjuice Potion [to break into Gringotts Bank] and gets to look like Bellatrix...Rather than put Emma Watson in a [lot] of make-up they just said, 'Now you go act like Hermione.' That was fun, because I always wanted to be Hermione. It was great fun; looking at Dan and Rupert and they were treating me as if I was seventeen."

BATTLE OF HOGWARTS

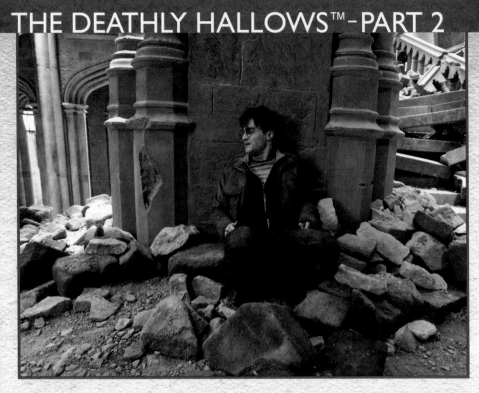

The final battle scenes were a lot of work to shoot, but the cast and crew were confident that fans would love them as much as they did! "Unquestionably more exciting and more substantial as well…the final half an hour, or the final hour, really, of the last film is going to be nonstop carnage," said Tom Felton.

last film as well because it really helps you when you're acting to think, 'This is the last one,' and literally it's all coming to this one point."

"It really brings home the magnitude of the sacrifice that Hermione and Ron make for Harry and for their friendship…. **Under these extraordinary circumstances, when everyone's life is on the line, they turn into these incredible kind of heroes,**" said Emma Watson.

"We're seeing the destruction of these sets, these buildings that have been with us since the beginning," said Matthew Lewis. "The Great Hall, the courtyards and stuff, and they're all getting wrecked. So it's been quite interesting as an actor to take all that on board. It's quite good it's the

Saying good-bye to their iconic roles was especially bitter-sweet for Daniel, Emma, and Rupert. They would never trade their time in the world of *Harry Potter*, but as they move on to the next chapters of their lives, their fans are incredibly excited to see what they'll do next!

"Potter is never something I would want to distance myself from because I'm incredibly proud of it, and it's given me the most amazing opportunities and I've met some of the most fantastic people and got to work with these brilliant actors," said Daniel Radcliffe. "But I certainly, obviously, want to establish myself as an actor in my own right rather than being just the actor who plays Harry Potter."

"It was kind of a weird experience trying to make the whole growing-up process run smoothly," said Emma Watson. "We kind of had to do it without anyone realizing. I don't know — we don't really think about it. Everyone always asks this question, 'Is it really hard growing up onscreen?' And I'm just like, 'Well, I've never grown up any other way, so I don't know.' It's just the way it's always been and you just kind of deal with it, I guess."

"For me, [filming the *Harry Potter* movies] just feels like it's just been one long experience, really, because it didn't really feel like that long," said Rupert Grint. "It's only when you look back on the first ones that you sort of realize how much we've grown up. And it's been really fun, though. I've enjoyed sort of every moment of it, so it's been really cool."

Index of Citations

Page 5

David Heyman quote:
Harry Potter and the Sorcerer's Stone film – DVD Disc 2 – Interviews

Stuart Craig quote:
Harry Potter and the Sorcerer's Stone film –DVD Disc 2 – Interviews

Chris Columbus quote:
Time for Kids "Potter Power! Celebrity Q&A: The Stars Speak Out"

Pages 6-7

Daniel Radcliffe
First quote:
PBS.org / *David Copperfield* / Essays & Interview / Daniel Radcliffe

Second quote:
CBBC Newsround / TV FILM / "Daniel Radcliffe: Full Interview," October 24, 2002

Third quote:
The Leaky Cauldron / "*Prisoner of Azkaban* Set Report: The Kids"

Fourth quote:
Scholastic.com / *Scholastic News* / "Daniel Radcliffe Talks About the Changes in Harry's Life"

Pages 8-9

Emma Watson
First quote:
Interview magazine / "Emma Watson"

Second quote:
CBBC Newsround / TV FILM / "Emma Watson *Chamber of Secrets*: Full Interview," November 11, 2002

Pages 10-11

Rupert Grint
First quote:
CBBC Newsround / TV FILM / "Rupert Grint: Full Interview," October 24, 2002

Second quote:
Scholastic.com / *Scholastic News* / "Rupert Grint"

Third quote:
Scholastic.com / *Scholastic News* / "Rupert Grint Has Fun Making the New Movie"

Pages 12-13

David Heyman quote:
Harry Potter and the Sorcerer's Stone film –DVD Disc 2 – Interviews

Tom Felton quote:
CBBC Newsround / TV FILM / "*Azkaban* Exclusives: Tom Felton," May 23, 2004

Katie Leung quote:
Scholastic.com / *Scholastic News* / Scholastic.com / "Harry's First Kiss!" July 16, 2007

Robert Pattinson quote:
CBBC Newsround / TV FILM / "NR Chats to *GOF*'s Robert Pattinson," November 15, 2005

Evanna Lynch quote:
IrishCentral.com / "Irish 'Luna Lovegood' on '*Harry Potter and the Half-Blood Prince*,'" June 11, 2009

Pages 14-15

Ralph Fiennes quote:
Variety.com / "Ralph Fiennes' constant shape-shifting," October 8, 2008

Alan Rickman quote:
Harry Potter Chamber of Secrets film, DVD Disc 2 – Behind Hogwarts

Michael Gambon quote:
SFGate.com / "Old '*Harry Potter*' wizard wise about movies," July 17, 2009

Robbie Coltrane quote:
Time for Kids / "Potter Power! Reporters' Journal: On the Scene at the Big Premiere"

David Bradley quote:
Harry Potter Chamber of Secrets film, DVD Disc 2 – Behind Hogwarts

Pages 16-17

Emma Watson quote:
The Leaky Cauldron / Video / Emma Watson PS Interview (2001)

First Daniel Radcliffe quote:
Nickelodeon magazine / Harry Potter feature / October 2001

Rupert Grint quote:
CBBC Newsround / TV FILM / "Rupert Grint: Full Interview," October 24, 2002

Second Daniel Radcliffe quote:
CBBC Newsround / TV FILM / "Daniel Radcliffe: Full Interview," October 24, 2002

Pages 18-19

Emma Watson quote:
CBBC Newsround / TV FILM / "Emma Watson: Full Interview," October 24, 2002

Daniel Radcliffe quote:
CBBC Newsround / Harry Potter Actors / Daniel Radcliffe (Harry), July 7, 2010

Rupert Grint quote:
CBBC Newsround / TV FILM / "Rupert Grint: Full Interview," October 24, 2002

Pages 20-21

David Heyman quote:
Harry Potter and the Sorcerer's Stone film – DVD Disc 2 – Interviews

First Daniel Radcliffe quote:
CBBC Newsround / TV FILM / "Daniel Radcliffe: Full Interview," October 24, 2002

Rupert Grint quote:
Nickelodeon magazine interview, October 2001

Second Daniel Radcliffe quote:
Time for Kids / "Potter Power! Celebrity Q&A: The Stars Speak Out"

Pages 22-23

Chris Columbus quote:
Harry Potter and the Sorcerer's Stone film – DVD
Disc 2 – Interviews

Stuart Craig quote:
Harry Potter and the Sorcerer's Stone film –DVD
Disc 2 – Interviews

Page 25

Chris Columbus quote:
The Leaky Cauldron / *Harry Potter and the Chamber of Secrets* / Chris Columbus Interview, October 22, 2002

Rupert Grint quote:
Scholastic.com / *Scholastic News* / "Rupert Grint"

John Richardson quote:
The Telegraph / "'*Harry Potter and the Half-Blood Prince*': A Kind of Magic," July 6, 2009

Pages 26-27

Rupert Grint quotes:
Scholastic.com / *Scholastic News* / "Rupert Grint"

Daniel Radcliffe quotes:
CBBC Newsround / TV FILM / *Chamber of Secrets* press conference, October 25, 2002

Pages 28-29

Rupert Grint quote:
Scholastic.com / *Scholastic News* / "Rupert Grint Has Fun Making the New Movie"

David Heyman quote:
The Telegraph / "More Mr. Nice Guy," June 23, 2007

First Daniel Radcliffe quote:
The Telegraph / "More Mr. Nice Guy," June 23, 2007

Second Daniel Radcliffe quote:
BBC.co.uk / BBC Films – Daniel Radcliffe, Emma Watson and Rupert Grint

Emma Watson quote:
The Leaky Cauldron / "*Prisoner of Azkaban* Set Report: The Kids"

Pages 30-31

Emma Watson quote:
The Leaky Cauldron / "*Prisoner of Azkaban* Set Report: The Kids"

Gary Gero quotes:
Scholastic.com / *Scholastic News* / "Animal Magic: Meet Gary Gero, Animal Trainer for Two *Harry Potter* Movies"

Daniel Radcliffe quote:
The Leaky Cauldron / "*Prisoner of Azkaban* Set Report: The Kids"

Pages 32-33

Tom Felton quote:
CBBC Newsround / TV FILM / "*Azkaban* Exclusives: Tom Felton," May 23, 2004

First Daniel Radcliffe quote:
The Leaky Cauldron / "*Prisoner of Azkaban* Set Report: The Kids"

Rupert Grint quote:
CBBC Newsround / TV FILM / "Hairy potter? NR talks to Rupert Grint"

Second Daniel Radcliffe quote:
The Leaky Cauldron / "*Prisoner of Azkaban* Set Report: The Kids"

Pages 34-35

Rupert Grint quote:
Scholastic.com / *Scholastic News* / "Rupert Grint as Ron Weasley in *Harry Potter and the Goblet of Fire*"

Robert Pattinson quotes:
CBBC Newsround / TV FILM / "NR Chats to *GOF*'s Robert Pattinson," November 15, 2005

Pages 36-37

All quotes:
Animation World Network / "*Harry Potter and the Goblet of Fire* — Wizard Competitions, Death Eaters and Voldemort," November 30, 2005

Page 38

Robert Pattinson quote:
CBBC Newsround / TV FILM / "NR Chats to *GOF*'s Robert Pattinson," November 15, 2005

Emma Watson quote:
MuggleNet / MuggleCast / Transcripts / *Goblet of Fire* Press Junket — The Trio, October 22, 2005

Pages 39-41

David Yates quote:
HowStuffWorks.com / "The Crew of Harry Potter 5"

Emma Watson quote:
Scholastic.com / *Scholastic News* / "An Interview with Hermione Granger," July 16, 2007

Evanna Lynch quote:
IrishCentral.com / "Irish 'Luna Lovegood' on '*Harry Potter and the Half-Blood Prince*,'" June 11, 2009

Matthew Lewis quote:
Scholastic.com / *Scholastic News* / "Neville Longbottom Fights Back," July 16, 2007

Pages 42-43

Daniel Radcliffe quotes:
Scholastic.com / *Scholastic News* / "Daniel Radcliffe Talks Harry Potter," July 16, 2007

Matthew Lewis quote:
Scholastic.com / *Scholastic News* / "Neville Longbottom Fights Back," July 16, 2007

Nick Dudman quotes:
HowStuffWorks.com / "Inside *Harry Potter and the Order of the Phoenix*: Prosthetic Makeup, Organic Props and More"

Pages 44-45:

Daniel Radcliffe quotes:
Scholastic.com / *Scholastic News* / "Daniel Radcliffe Talks Harry Potter," July 16, 2007

Katie Leung quote:
Scholastic.com / *Scholastic News* / Scholastic.com / "Harry's First Kiss!" July 16, 2007

Pages 46-47

First Bonnie Wright quote:
The *Daily Mail* Online: "How Bonnie Charmed Harry," December 12, 2009

First Daniel Radcliffe quote:
MTV.com / "Daniel Radcliffe Credits 'Hormones' With *Harry Potter and the Half-Blood Prince* Success," December 7, 2009

First Rupert Grint quote:
Scholastic.com / *Scholastic News* / "Harry Potter Opens July 15," July 13, 2009

Second Rupert Grint quote:
ComingSoon.net / *"Harry Potter and the Half-Blood Prince* Set Visit: Rupert Grint," July 8, 2009

Second Daniel Radcliffe quote:
MovieWeb.com / *"Harry Potter and the Half-Blood Prince* Cast Interviews," July 13, 2009

Second Bonnie Wright quote:
Time for Kids / "TFK Chats with Bonnie Wright," July 15, 2009

Pages 48-49

Emma Watson quote:
MovieWeb.com / *"Harry Potter and the Half-Blood Prince* Cast Interviews," July 13, 2009

Bonnie Wright quotes:
Time for Kids / "TFK Chats with Bonnie Wright," July 15, 2009

Tom Felton quote:
MovieWeb.com / *"Harry Potter and the Half-Blood Prince* Cast Interviews," July 13, 2009

Daniel Radcliffe quote:
MovieWeb.com / *"Harry Potter and the Half-Blood Prince* Cast Interviews," July 13, 2009

Warwick Davis quote:
Scholastic.com / *Scholastic News* / "Harry Potter Opens July 15," July 13, 2009

Page 50

David Heyman quote:
Scholastic.com / *Scholastic News* / "Harry Potter Opens July 15," July 13, 2009

Tim Alexander quote:
The Los Angeles Times Hero Boy / *"Harry Potter* Countdown: Scaring Up the Inferi," June 18, 2009

Pages 51-52

Bonnie Wright quote:
MTV.com / *"Harry Potter and the Deathly Hallows* Set Is 'Absolute Madness,' Daniel Radcliffe Says," December 8, 2009

Emma Watson quote:
CNN.com / *"Half-Blood Prince* finds Potter crew closer to end," July 14, 2009

Matthew Lewis quote:
SnitchSeeker.com / "Chris Rankin & Matthew Lewis Talk *Deathly Hallows* to SnitchSeeker," April 14, 2010

Daniel Radcliffe quote:
MovieWeb.com / *"Harry Potter and the Half-Blood Prince* Cast Interviews," July 13, 2009

Page 52

David Yates quote:
MovieWeb.com / "First *Harry Potter and the Deathly Hallows* Team Photo Arrives," December 1, 2009

Daniel Radcliffe quote:
CBBC Newsround / TV FILM / "Action-Packed *Potter* on the way," December 1, 2009

Rupert Grint quote:
MovieWeb.com / "First *Harry Potter and the Deathly Hallows* Team Photo Arrives," December 1, 2009

Pages 54-55

David Yates quote:
MTV.com / *"Harry Potter* Producer Says *Deathly Hallows* Will Be 'Even More Epic' in 3-D," March 29, 2010

Evanna Lynch quote:
IrishCentral.com / "Evanna Lynch Psyched for Next *Harry Potter* Movie," December 20, 2009

Matthew Lewis quote:
LatinoReview.com / "Chris Rankin & Matthew Lewis Talk About *Deathly Hallows*," April 15, 2010

Pages 57-58

Rupert Grint quote:
CBBC Newsround / TV FILM / "Action-Packed *Potter* on the way," December 1, 2009

Emma Watson quote:
MovieWeb.com / *"Harry Potter and the Half-Blood Prince* Cast Interviews," July 13, 2009

Evanna Lynch quote:
IrishCentral.com / "Evanna Lynch Psyched for Next *Harry Potter* Movie," December 20, 2009

Helena Bonham Carter quote:
MTV.com / "Helena Bonham Carter Enjoyed Impersonating Hermione in *Deathly Hallows*," February 23, 2010

Pages 58-59

Tom Felton quote:
The Leaky Cauldron / "Tom Felton: 'Non-Stop Carnage' for Last Hour of *Deathly Hallows*," April 17, 2010

Matthew Lewis quote:
SnitchSeeker.com / "Chris Rankin & Matthew Lewis Talk *Deathly Hallows* to SnitchSeeker," April 14, 2010

Emma Watson quote:
MovieWeb.com / Video: *"Harry Potter and the Deathly Hallows* Story Featurette," August 11, 2010

Page 61

All quotes:
Hollywood.com / "A Spell-binding Chat with *Harry Potter*'s Daniel Radcliffe, Emma Watson and Rupert Grint," July 12, 2007